The Recluse

Victor Reardon

Copyright © 2021 Victor Reardon

Edited by Ian Sputnik
Cover illustration by Pete Linforth/ Pixabay

ISBN: 9798592398544

Dedication

For Ben.
You were the best of us.

Contents

Acknowledgements

I remember being fourteen years old and I would sit on the porch with my friend K. Her mum would make me a hot drink and we would sit on that old rocking chair under the stars and talk about all the things in life we planned on doing.

It's been ten years and those plans went out the window as life took over - as it does.

I crossed one thing off that list.

For Ian Sputnik, for helping me in every way possible in getting this done. I'm grateful.
If anything, I'll get you the first pint.

For Becs, for putting up with my nonsense and being with me every step of the way; for the encouragement and support.

The Long Drive

"There is a hockey-masked killer right here in Wakefield and what are we doing?" Tom asked, holding up a newspaper to his uninterested driver.

It had become almost like a ritual now. Tom almost every morning would go through the gazette with John, often discussing the local news throughout Wakefield. Although the town was small there was rarely a dull day. It was a town almost famous for its diverse catalogue of inhabitants coming from all over the world to explore its rich history.

"No seriously, we are driving a hundred fucking miles to talk to an old lady about why she stopped making movies."

"Because that's just it, mate. She made seven movies, seven big movies in a year. You know the only people that make that many films a year are porn stars," John replied, gripping the wheel to his beat-up old Ford; the sun bearing down heavily.

There were always a few things you could count on during these long journeys between interviews that took up a large part of their day. The first being the abundance of food hidden in the car by Tom. The second, that on more than one occasion Tom would pull out his camera and tinker with it more than necessary. Lastly, the drives were long and often at times hard.

"Then she gets married, makes another six movies; then one her husband is murdered, stabbed eighty-six times! can you imagine that? She's held down and forced to watch as her husband is fucking swiss cheesed," John said glancing over to Tom wincing; for all his bravado and depravity there was a level of violence that unsettled him.

"I'm a lover not a fighter, and a pretty good lover," he would often joke.

"How are things with Charlie?" John asked looking over to Tom who had begun piling up snacks onto his lap.

"Things are really good," Tom said as he clutched the green emerald ring that hung from his neck.

"Listen there's something I wanted to talk about before we get to this place. It was two years last month since your sister passed and I know you booked the time off and since you've been back, I've barely seen you. I just wanted to make sure you were good."

John took a second and cleared his throat, looking at the road ahead intently.

"I'm good," he lied. "She was in a lot of pain for a long time and I know she's in a better place."

The drive through Wakefield had been a long one. Tom and John knew what this job meant as much as they joked about it. It had made the pressure easier to deal with.

Mary Celeste had been a recluse for the best part of forty years. No one had known why she had suddenly chosen to talk after all this time.

The offices of the Wakefield gazette had pooled a bet to see which one the guys would fuck it up first or be kicked out. Would Tom say something vulgar and offend her or would John get far too personal?

Victor Reardon

Mary Celeste

John pulled into the long gravel driveway of Mrs Celeste's beaten old house. The driveway was long and overgrown. They pulled up about forty feet from the front door. As they pulled in, they admired the marble stonewall podiums which sat on each side of the giant barricade-like front door. The small square windows that sat in rows of three covering the top half were filled in with wood and nailed over, blocking the view into the house.

Looking around they noticed all the surrounding windows were covered in the same manner.

Standing at around five foot eight John was athletic and considered good looking by most. His eyes were a bright shade of green and his hair a dark brown.

Stepping out of the vehicle John had made sure not to let the dusty gravel scuff his shoes. Although not too vain, he'd always believed that it was important to make a good first impression and this was done through presentation.

John took a notepad from a rucksack that he'd grabbed from the back seat and begun taking notes on the house.

Tom stood a little small at five foot five. He weighed noticeably more than John but would always say "it's muscle" if anyone had made digs about his smaller but heavier stature.

A little more relaxed than John, Tom opted to wear jeans and a shirt over Johns more formal ensemble. Around his neck, he wore a thin silver necklace that held a beautiful green emerald ring that hung just low enough to rest against his chest. Tom lit a cigarette and looked up to the sky; taking a moment to enjoy the sun beaming down on his face.

Walking up the Indian sandstone steps that were aged and cracked; Tom threw his cigarette back onto the gravel, gave John a nudge of excitement and knocked on the door.

As both gentlemen stood there waiting patiently, Tom had held his camera on a strap that hung from his neck.

"Smile," he said lifting it and snapping a picture of John, before taking more of the surrounding environment including the long driveway.

"Stand back and raise your hands. I want to see them," A voice shouted from behind the thick wooden fortress.

John took his notepad and threw it back into the rucksack and dropped it by his feet before raising his hands.

As both men held their hands high in the air they listened; confused looks on their faces as they could hear various locks and bolts turning on the other side of the door.

"What the fuck?" Tom mouthed to John.

The door opened a small crack as Mrs Celeste poked her head out sheepishly through the inch gap she had created.

Her eyes were a vibrant shade of blue. Like looking into the sky on a warm summer's day she winced them tight when the sunlight hit her; before stopping to feel the warmth on her face almost like it was the first time.

"The reporters?" she whispered looking over John's shoulder, scanning the environment as her hands trembled causing the large door and latch to rattle.

Tom looked in Johns direction, trying to see what Mrs Celeste was looking at before lifting his camera and taking another picture of John.

She rushed the men in quickly, keeping an eye on the front garden the entire time.

"Don't knock the salt," she snapped gesturing to the thick lining of salt that covered the width of the front door.

Immediately there was a sense of unease that surrounded them. Every window was blocked with a thick layer of solid wood and each door had a bell attached to it that rung through the house loudly when pressed.

She led them to a room centred in the middle of the house; a large circular room with no windows lit only by lamps. The walls were lined with books from the floor right to the ceiling. She slammed the heavy door behind her, bolting it shut with a single thick lock before motioning a hand in the direction of a single long chair so they could sit. From the moment they sat down Mrs Celeste did not take her eyes off John - almost enamoured with him she studied his words and movements intently.

"So, you were born Hill? How did you come up with the name Mary Celeste?"

"My great grandfather was a merchant, and growing up he had a whittled wooden version of the ship Mary Celeste. He placed it in front of a window in his home in New York and when the sun went down, he'd grab me and say "it's like being back out on the ocean."

She spoke erratically, bouncing between frantic and calm, unable to sit still. She pulled herself to the edge of her seat; looked at John and stared deep into his eyes.

She dragged her chair forward towards him. "What did you do?" she asked staring at John. "He hasn't been this lively in years."

"Who?" John asked looking around the room.

The room fell silent before Mrs Celeste ran her fingers through her thick greying blonde hair. She clapped her hands together and jumped out of her chair before running out of the room.

"So, this is going well," Tom whispered sarcastically to John, chuckling to himself. "Mate she's crazy. Let's get the fuck out of here before she comes back and murders us."

"We can't just run out the front door: (1) because she locked it, (2) because she's coming back."

She ran back into the room hopping with excitement, a wad of photos gripped tightly in her hand. She threw herself over the back of the sofa and landed comfortably and passed the photos to Tom.

They had sat with Mrs Celeste for hours as she recounted tales from her youth. She passed pictures around and told stories from her short-lived Hollywood career; from getting off the bus with less than fifty dollars that had been given to her by her mum, and a bag of clothes. To how she had met her husband during a call back in which she was asked to go topless.

She had refused - unless the three male casting agents agreed to go without their pants for the remainder of the interview. A move that would end with the director being called in and her winning the role.

She spoke about these days with excitement clear in her voice and bursts of energy as she bounced from memory to memory.

"I had been called in to audition for a superhero movie that was being directed by some art-house guy and I turned up with a cape borrowed by an actor friend of mine. Well, I turned up ready to, you know, deal out some justice. They wanted me to play the love interest. I was to be caught a lot; falling and screaming a lot! Apparently, a man that can fly and punches criminals made sense but a female superhero, they weren't ready for."

"Mrs Celeste."

"Call me Faith; that's my birth name," she said taking a breath to calm herself and sinking into her seat before slapping her hands together and pulling herself back to the front of the seat.

"I want to talk to you about the night your husband passed."

The room fell silent, the only noise was that of an old clock ticking away in the distance.

"What happened the night he passed?"

"I woke up in the early hours of the morning to what sounded like someone trying to break in. It was a loud banging that ran through the house and it scared me. So, I woke up my husband who grabbed a bat that he had kept under the bed and ran downstairs. He told me he'd call when everything was okay but he never did," She said, her voice breaking at the thought. "I waited and waited but he never called; so, I went to the top of the stairs and I called his name. He didn't respond, so I crept down the stairs. As I reached the bottom there was a thumping noise," she banged her hand together three times trying to replicate the noise.

"As I crept up and poked my head around the corner, he was lying there on the floor gurgling and spitting blood. I didn't see that... that monster was still stabbing him. I was so scared I just stared at him. That's when he saw me. I tried to run but I was frozen; have you ever been so scared that you can't move? I felt like a guest in my own body."

"That's when he came for me, he hit me so hard I fell and he pressed his foot hard on my head; one of the last things I remember is a boot on my face before that thing went back to my husband, grabbing a knife and plunging it into his heart."

"I looked into his eyes as they glazed over; that was the first time I ever saw my husband cry," she said grabbing a tissue and wiping the tears from her eyes.

John and Tom had talked about this night together plenty of times over beers at home. Its place in film history was discussed alongside others like Norma Jean and Sharon Tate. Having been told and retold over and over, it was easy to become lost in the mystery and forget that these were real people and the consequences of that night had affected so many throughout the film industry.

Hours passed discussing that night and her decision to move to Wakefield following the incident that had changed the course of her life.

They discussed the hows and the whys, the what-ifs and the regrets of what could have been with her career - not just a renowned actress but a singer known for being able to hold a room like a captive audience with a voice as near to angelic as one could be.

Coming from a time when women weren't leading cinema, Mrs Celeste fought for her place within the film industry - only to have it pulled out from beneath her.

John scribbled notes intently, hooked on every word that she said. It quickly became very clear how she'd managed to build her career so fast; each new story as captivating as the last.

"Faith, I have to ask, you said *he* hasn't been this lively in years, who is *he*?"

She took a second as her facial expression changed to that of anger and hurt as she pulled herself forward sitting onto the edge of her seat.

"He's the devil on your back, he's never ageing, never stopping and he knows you. He knows something that you did, something you aren't proud off," she took a second and looked deep into John's eyes.

"Did you hurt someone?"

John's eyes widened and his skin went pale. He put the notepad down. "I don't know what you are talking about."

"You can lie to me; yourself and your partner but you can't lie to him and I'm sorry, it's too late now."

Mr Heath & The Hooded Figure

"So, she's fucking nuts," Tom laughed, throwing his bags into the back on Johns car before calling shotgun and jumping into the passenger seat.

John was unable to shake the unease in the back of his mind. He checked the back seat and the boot of his car and would check the road behind him but the seeds of uncertainty and doubt had been planted in his mind running his blood cold.

"None of these photos came out properly, somethings blocking the lens. I'll have to get them developed properly, fuck it feels like the 90s," Tom complained, throwing the camera in the bag and putting it behind him.

He watched John while they were driving home. He could see his mind affected by the words she'd said. Tom had become quiet and distant.

As they approached John's home, they'd noticed a page torn from a legal pad stuck to his front door.

Tom pulled it off and read it out.

> *Dear neighbour*
> *I have asked you several times not to park in*
> *front of my house. I have warned you that the next*
> *time any damage that occurs I will not be taking*
> *responsibility for it.*

"He knows he's just admitted on paper that he's ready to commit criminal damage, right?" Tom joked.

The neighbour lived across the road. The only thing they'd known about him was his name, Heath.

He'd often hide behind a curtain and watch the people that lived around him; opting to communicate through sticky notes rather than in person. He'd watched the men pull up in their car from his window before ducking back behind the curtain.

John opened up the front door to be greeted by a gigantic white dog; blue-eyed and fluffy he had watched them from the window. John petted the dog before leading it through the house to the kitchen, swinging open the fridge and passing a Whitfields beer to Tom.

Whitfield's was a Welsh beer that was popular throughout Wakefield. As beads of condensation ran down the dark blue bottles, they cracked them open and both went silent as they enjoyed their first sips.

As John opened the back door to let Ollie out, he hit play on the answering machine and sat down with Tom to discuss the events of the day.

They had gone over the notes of the day and debated between them on whether to include her final crazy outburst or not before deciding to sleep on it.

Tom finished his beer before giving John a wink and a smile and leaving. As John let him out, he grabbed another bottle of beer and sat taking a moment to enjoy it before heading upstairs.

He pulled himself up and took a slow walk, almost dragging his now tired body along the landing before gently pushing the door open and standing at the foot of his bed.

He fell flat into the soft silk sheets and almost instantly fell asleep.

John could feel the cold running up his back as he looked up to the jet-black sky; noticing the absence of stars his minds raced listening to the voices in the darkness.

"He's coming," they whispered, he looked down at his feet and felt the wet ground being soaked up by his socks.

He tried to move but his legs were frozen stiff as the voices continued to ring out. He pulled up his hands and dropped the blood-soaked syringe that he had been gripping tightly.

The garden was so cold John could feel it slowly taking over his body as his fingers and toes began to numb. He tried to run but nothing worked, when all of a sudden, the wind stopped and he felt a warm breath on his neck.

"He found you," the voice in the distance called out.

John awoke in a panic, as a cold chill ran down his spine. He checked his watch and jumped out of bed checking that he hadn't overslept and missed Toms dinner.

He grabbed a blue shirt from his dresser and a tie to match, before hurrying down the stairs and getting a lead for Ollie.

"Did you get my note?" A voice shouted from across the road. Tall and skinny heath stood at a distance; a smug look covering his face.

He stood with his arms crossed making sure to keep at least one foot inside the threshold.

"You gonna move your car?"

Hearing this John put his keys back into his pocket before walking off into the distance smiling to himself. Heath had done his best to alienate those who lived closest to him. He had become a mystery.

Although John was sure Heath had a daughter or a niece; he thought he'd seen someone going in once or twice, but he couldn't be sure.

Heath stood in his doorway his veiny arms still crossed tightly as he watched John walk off into the unknown.

"What are you looking at?" he snapped at the hooded figure that had appeared on the other side of the small brick wall that separated the front garden and the stone pathway that divided the houses on the street.

The hooded figure looked off in the direction which John had walked, then looked back at

Heath. Unfazed he just stared; tilting his head slightly.

Seeing that John had moved out of sight Heath ran back inside, grabbed a notepad and began scribbling.

> *I have asked many times for you not to park your car in my space.*
>
> *If you carry on or threaten me again, I will seek legal action and I will be calling animal services on your untrained, vicious mutt.*

He ripped it from the pad and made his way over to John's front door; moving past the hooded figure. He stuck it on the door and ran back to his front garden.

"Seriously what the fuck are you doing?" Heath snapped at the still figure, who without hesitation made his way towards him, leaping the front wall rapidly before knocking him down with a thunderous elbow to the head.

Hitting the concrete hard, Heath could instantly feel warm blood pulsing from the back of his head. He reached up towards it and retched upon feeling the bone protruding from his skull.

Panicking he rolled onto his front and begun desperately trying to claw his way up the patio to the safety of his house.

The hooded figure stopped and stood tall, watching patiently as Heath dragged himself across the pavement, his blood-soaked hands slapping against the wet pavement. Before he could make his way any further, he felt a vice-like grip around his ankle pulling him back.

"Let go of me," he cried.

The figure gripped his hands tightly around Heath's head and stared deeply into his eyes before squeezing with an almighty forced. Feeling a tight crack run through his head like thunder, Heath screamed as his eyes cried tears of blood.

Heath attempted in vain to push back his attacker. His hands pressed against the immovable chest of the hooded nightmare. As his screams died, Heath pleaded weakly. The hooded nightmare moved his hands around his throat and gripping tightly with his thumbs buried deep in Heath's neck, almost inverting his Adam's apple. Never breaking eye contact, the figure stared deeply in Heath's eyes watching the life fade slowly.

Heath's eyes rolled back as he fell unconscious. The hooded man moved his hands so that they were pressed firmly against either side of heath's head and with one swift motion snapped his neck, before standing tall and stomping down as hard as possible smashing Heath's head in two. He raised his leg once again and stamped it down again, this time hitting the concrete underneath Heath, throwing bone fragments and brain across the garden.

He lifted his boot and stomped again and again; and once more before he looked up into the direction that John had walked off in; putting his hands in his pockets and taking a quiet stroll into the night.

Friends

John made his way to Tom's unaware of the events that had occurred after he had left home, making sure to stop and enjoy the cold night air. He tapped on the door and took a step back as Ollie sat down next him. They waited before the front door swung open revealing a half tipsy Tom grinning like a Cheshire cat.

"You alright mate?" Tom smiled leaning down to stroke Ollie who had sat patiently wagging and waiting. John followed Tom straight through to the wide-open living room where a nice cold Whitfields was waiting for him.

"Thank you bud," John parked himself down and smiled.

"Where's your lady friend?"

"She's out back fixing that bloody grill," Tom said, cracking the top the beer and holding the bottle lid, jumped into the adjoining seat.

"Okay so I've spoken to Maude and the story is good to go out within the next few days, but I found something I wanted you to look at."

Tom reached down to the side off the sofa and pulled out a small stack of paperwork.

John took it from Tom; placed the beer to the side of him and opened it stunned.

"Damn!"

"So, it turns out Mrs Celeste's husband had a history of violence with multiple women throughout his career and numerous incidents on set with actresses."

"She never said anything."

"Right! However, there is one witness that claims he once struck her on set."

"Why didn't she tell us?"

"I'm not sure. I've been trying to contact her but she hasn't been responding. Also got a few more jobs to chase tomorrow. You wanna hear the options?"

"Hit me."

"Okay," Tom said, smiling and pulling out another stack of files he had previously been using as a beer mat.

"Here are our options. There's a guy in the city who reckons he's got photos of superheroes on rooftops."

"I'm sorry, what?"

"Or...we are on the door for Saf's, the new eatery that allegedly serves the best steak on the entire planet."

"No, no, no. Don't just gloss over that... superheroes?"

"Some nutjob wearing hockey pads. It's not even worth our time! Steak...whiskey...steak, come on man."

John just smiled "Steak sound's good."

"There is no way you guys are talking about work whilst I'm out there busting my chops over that bloody grill."

Charlie stood in the doorway with a hand on her hip and a Whitfield's in the other. She stood tall with jet black dark hair and piercing bright eyes, one green one blue.

"You didn't need my help... your words," Tom chuckled - throwing the bottle lid clutched in his hand into the small wooden bin sat on the opposite side of the room.

It missed.

"I didn't need you to punch the side of the grill like a drunk Fonzy. No, you're right, but I did get it working."

"So, no more work talk, and chops outside," Charlie smiled, cracking off the top of her bottle and throwing it in the same bin.

It landed.

John walked out through the backdoor and was instantly hit by the smell of sizzling meat and spice; smoked paprika filled the cool night air.

He sat himself down and stroked Ollie who had made his way out to sit next to him.

Charlie rushed out of the backdoor giggling; Tom followed behind quickly and wrapped his arms around her, picking her up and spinning her; before she could untuck his arms and get behind him still holding the beer high so as to not drop it.

They playfully wrestled until they came crashing down into the chair together and took a breath.

"So, Charlie what do you do?"

"I work for GhostApple."

"The virtual reality company?"

"Yeah, I'm assuming Tom didn't give you the tickets I gave him."

"Tickets?"

"Why am I not surprised? Thomas didn't tell you I got you both tickets to the beta test of our newest game?"

"In my defence...I forgot," Tom laughed taking a sip of beer.

"That's not a good defence."

"And we've been dealing with a crazy woman for most of today."

Tom stood up; took the food from the grill and handed each person a plate before sitting down himself to eat.

"Yeah, so what's her deal? From what Tom tells me she sounded a little out of it? Guess that's what happens when you don't communicate with people for so long. But I've been meaning to ask...who was she talking about?"

"I have no idea. She kept staring over John's shoulder like there was someone behind him."

"Wish you'd have told me that."

"Sorry bud," Tom said laughing.

"I told you she was crazy from the get-go."

"You are not wrong," John laughed.

"But something's kept her there. I just don't know what? you know?"

"Oh, I forgot to mention it," Tom said looking at John. "I've booked some time off in March; Charlie and I are going to Sudan."

"Pardon? what's in Sudan?"

"Tom is going to meet my parents," Charlie said smiling and putting a hand on Tom's leg.

"Wow!" John replied, surprised.

"How you gonna explain this man child to your parents?" He laughed.

"I thought about that."

"Babe!" Tom interjected.

"But my dad's pretty cool; he loves that I'm out here making video games. He wanted to come out to us, but we just weren't able to make it work."

"I'm really happy for you guys; it's nice to see him trying to act mature for a change," John laughed pointing a thumb at Tom and giving him a cheeky wink.

"It's gonna be you next, mate," Tom opined, grabbing another beer.

"Who needs a partner when I've got this one?" John chuckled, reaching an arm over and patting Ollie softly on the side.

"Okay bud; are you gonna be alright?" Tom laughed walking a now drunk John to the front door.

"I'm fine," he slurred; holding Ollie's lead in one hand and stumbling out of the front door into the cold night air.

"Do me a favour mate, when you get home text me a message."

"I've got you. Thank you for tonight; sorry mate," John apologised, almost stumbling over a hooded passer-by.

"Pisshead," Tom chuckled looking at John confused and shutting the door.

Alex

Stumbling home, John stopped under an overly bright-lit lamp post as he leaned against it, trying to keep some semblance of balance and let out Ollie's lead a little.

"Go on boy," he said as Ollie, who was trying to find a suitable place to pee. "Take your time," he chuckled.

John pulled out his phone and scrolled through Twitter; occasionally looking over the top to keep an eye on Ollie.

Turning the screen black, John noticed a reflection over his shoulder; a reflection dark and menacing, a hooded figure stared deep into his eyes; its own eyes red like fire.

He turned around instantly but the area was clear; silent and lit only by street lights. The only noise was from the occasional car in the distance.

John pulled his phone back up in front of his face and immediately locked eyes with a figure in the darkness. Time stopped and they looked deep into each other's eyes for what seemed like a lifetime.

"Nope," he chuckled, putting his phone back into his pocket.

"I may have drunk too much buddy," He said to Ollie smiling.

John turned the corner to his road and was instantly met with flashing lights and sirens.

"I'm sorry sir there has been an incident do you live on this road?"

"Yes sir," He slurred, looking over the stern officer's shoulder at the now busy road, filled with various shades of flashing lights and officers trying their best to stop people from being nosey and to hide the blood and brains that had run into the road like a burst pipe.

"If you don't mind, I'm just going to walk you down to your door."

"Of course, officer, lead the way."

Following the policeman down the path, he took John's details and filled him in on the situation.

"Do you know anyone that would have any problems with Mr Cairn?"

"Yeah, everyone on this road would be a decent start?"

The officer looked down at the length of the road and sighed.

"Everyone?"

"Oh yeah," John answered, pulling the note attached to his door and passing it to the officer.

"Here you go."

"This is from him?"

"Yep, I usually get at least two of these a day," he slurred.

"Okay Mr Mason, you get some sleep and I'm going to stop by in the morning and talk to you properly."

"Yessir," John slurred, stumbling through the front door and almost tripping over in the process.

Staggering up the stairs, John pulled his phone out and dialled Tom.

"You alright pisshead?"

"Yeah, I need a massive favour."

"Go for it, brother," Tom said, Charlie giggling in the background.

"Loo's like Heath was attacked; reckon you could make a few calls and get us the details on what happened?"

"Shit son, is he okay? yeah, I'll make a few calls see what I can dig up?"

"No mate; he's dead."

"Couldn't have happened to a nicer prick," Tom scoffed.

"Listen, mate, get some sleep I've got to go."

"See you later brother."

Stumbling upstairs, slowly pulling off his clothes as he fumbled and banged into everything along the way.

John walked into the bathroom, ran cold water and splashed it into his face; sobering up as the cold water hit him, he looked into the mirror the see the veins along his neck had now spread thicker and further.

Now a luminous shade of blue; John ran his hands along his neck to feel the blood pumping heavy.

"What the f…" he thought to himself; turning back and walking back into his bedroom; before John's head hit the pillow, he was out.

Awaking to a familiar pink room, John looked down at his hands that were covered in blood - dripping on the soft blue carpet his left hand gripped an empty syringe.

"Johnny?"

John looked up to see Alex laying in her bed; hooked up with tubes and machines pumping away. The electrocardiogram attached to her was flatlining loudly almost drowning out Alex's sobs.

"Alex!" John screamed, guilt and anxiety filling his heart - making it hard for him to breath.

"Johnny!" She cried; tears of blood running down her cheeks.

"What's happening?"

"Johnny, he won't let me go."

"I'm so sorry."

John's chest got tighter and tighter and it became harder to breathe.

"Johnny you have to listen to me…he's coming," she cried.

"He knows what you did! You need to run...run and hide please."

Alex began pulling at the wires that were attached to her; ripping and tugging out the tubes ripping skin from her arms in the process and spraying blood across the room.

John awoke in a state of panic, cold sweat running down his back; he could see the silhouette of the door lit dimly by streetlights.

He tried desperately to move but felt as if he was being held down; pressure pushing down on his chest as it tightened like a vice. Turning slowly, he stared at the door unable to move...paralyzed with fear as his pillow moistened.

When he awoke, tears streamed down his cheeks, his face now cold and wet.

'It was like she was there; she was so real,' John thought to himself. Now his hands were finally his own again and he could move. He pulled himself up out of bed; dragged his half numb body into his bathroom; ran the cold tap and threw a handful of water into his face instantly bringing him back to life.

Looking at his reflection in the mirror, John could see the blue veins that were on his neck were now luminous - running from the length of his neck up to his chin. John reached up and ran his hand along them.

"Arghh!" he let out a gasp of pain; the sting was instant and vicious.

John's eyes were bloodshot and his skin was now beginning to pale - contrasting against the brightness of the blue and red now running up his neck.

'I'm losing my mind' John thought to himself.

'Maybe I've been drinking too much?'

Since Alex had passed, it had felt like the only thing that dumbed the pain and guilt; although he did try to throw himself into his work there were only so many stories he could chase or nights he could sit in front a computer.

Just one.

Maybe another.

We've all done it. We make excuses for our weaknesses and tell ourselves a little won't hurt; destructive by nature.

And now Alex was gone and she wasn't coming back.

There were many nights John found himself sat on the old sofa watching those old comic book and space movies that Alex used to love on the nights they sat together; John asking questions, not understanding - but it made Alex happy at that's what mattered.

He'd sit alone, looking over to that space now occupied only by an old bootleg StarFire blanket; her favourite character; folded neatly, untouched.

"Ollie!" John called out.

Victor Reardon

The Assault

Walking through the living room and opening the back door on the way through to let Ollie out; John walked through to the kitchen and poured himself a coffee; as Ollie ran out excitedly into the darkness.

John sat for a moment, the steaming cup in his hand - letting the warmth run through his fingers and enjoying the smell; he took a second - closed his eyes and forgot about the world.

Out of the blackness of the garden came along screeching howl that was quickly silenced.

John put down the mug and ran straight through the open door into the night.

He was stopped in his tracks when stood halfway down the garden, the hooded figure held Ollie by the throat.

Ollie hung lifeless. The figure threw the dog down and took off in John's direction, running rapidly. Before John could turn and run, he was struck hard; falling back, his head bounced hard off the concrete.

John looked up to see the figure moving towards him. He raised a leg and attempted to kick the figure. Before he could, his leg was swiped and he was struck against the head again.

He turned onto his stomach and began crawling away. His blood-soaked hands slapped across the pavement.

John felt a tight grip against his ankle; he stopped and turned around to see the figure pulling him back.

Looking across the garden he could see Ollie's white fur now red - barely visible in the darkness; John threw another desperate kick breaking the grip that was latched onto his leg and hobbled to his feet.

He raised his balled, bloody fists to his chin and began swinging wildly at the figure who seemed to relish this moment - now grinning ear to ear, he took a step back and then threw himself wildly at John, taking each punch before throwing his own back.

Struggling to catch his breath, John slowed down as his arms began to tire and fall from his chin, John dropped to a knee as blood dripped into a puddle on the ground below him.

The figure stood tall in front of him, took a knee in front of John and put one hand under his chin, raised it slightly so they could be eye level and for a moment time stopped as John froze with fear.

"Who are you?" he asked, his voice trembling; tears running down his cheeks.

The figure stood back onto his feet, gripped John's neck with one hand and with the other took a hard swing splattering blood along the fence behind him.

The hand wrapped around John's throat now tighter; then both hands. He squeezed hard as John tried to push him off, clawing and scratching, trying anything desperately to end the merciless beating.

Everything started to go black before Ollie, out of nowhere, threw himself at the hooded figure - biting hard and latching onto his arm.

John got to his feet, his legs shaking; barely able to keep himself up. He turned and ran for the back door. Throwing himself through the doorway; he turned around as Ollie ran through after him. He quickly locked the door.

The hooded figure stood on the other side of the door and stared at John; his chest was beating fast and he was enraged.

They locked eyes for a moment before the figure turned and walked back into the darkness.

John took a long breath...and passed out.

Victor Reardon

Amour

"Johnny come on, wake up," John awoke to Alex pushing his chest; she jabbed at him with one of her crutches.

"Come on it's my birthday, wake up," She pushed and pushed whilst using her cane to keep some form of balance.

"You should be in your chair."

"True, but the cane makes me look like an absolute badass? I'm not sure why. Is it a weapon? Does it have a sword in the stick? Who knows?"

"Back to your room, before I remove the stick and take the wheels off your chair."

"Mean...it's called a FabMobile" she chuckled turning around and making her way out of the room.

"So that makes you...Fabman?"

"Fabwoman...come on Alfred it's time for breakfast."

"Oh, I'm the butler? Wow, that hurts," he laughed to himself jumping out of bed and getting ready.

"The butler."

As he made his way downstairs, Alex was already set up at the breakfast table; she sat there smiling with a small stack of comics she was flipping through.

"What are you reading this morning?" John asked grabbing bits out of the fridge and checking dates on ingredients.

"Milk goes out today so I guess I'm making pancakes?"

"I mean why aren't they already made?" Alex chuckled "Come on butler," She laughed clapping her hands together.

"And I am reading the spectacular adventures of the coffee woman."

"I'm sorry? It's exactly what it sounds like...so when she drinks coffee, she gains the strength of the coffee that she drinks."

"Wow!"

"And her main villain is Tea-man..."

"No?"

"Who is her brother."

"I love it."

"Right put those away," he instructed, putting down a plate of maple-soaked pancakes with some crispy bacon on top and a golden hash brown on the side."

"I am the butler..."

"Ha-ha, yeah you are," She laughed tucking in.

"Right let's go," John said, wrapping a scarf around Alex who was sat comfortably in her chair and wheeling her out of the door.

"You know if you got me a paddle, I could move this chair around like a canoe and freak people out in the process," Alex said mimicking paddling a canoe with her hands and smiling back at John.

"As amazing as that would be, I don't think I'm gonna allow that."

"Fun sponge," she said still swinging her arms around.

Alex sat in her chair wrapped tight in a thick blue Jumper; she had short blonde hair that was shaved on one side, bright green eyes and vibrant red lips; dimples in her cheeks that were surrounded by tiny freckles that covered most of her face.

She was short and underweight; a result of her condition but had an appetite that often scared the people around her. She loved food and felt a sense of gratitude that although she wouldn't wish her condition on anyone as it was often painful, she loved having the excuse to eat as much as possible.

"So, is Tom going to be at dinner with us?"

"No...is someone crushing?" John chuckled.

"Yes, and I've made no effort to hide that," she replied, looking back and giving John a wink.

"Not okay with any of that. Anyway, I'm sorry bud Tom's out of town...you know it would never work out?"

"Why's that?"

"Because I'd kill him," John said trying his hardest to sound somewhat tough.

"Hmm, I think he'd kick your ass."

"I used to box you know."

"Everyone used to box bro! and I was there I remember you coming second A LOT!"

"Ouch!"

"He will be mine; you watch."

John unlocked the door and wheeled Alex through.

"Oh my god," Alex screamed with exhilaration, as the first thing she saw was Tom sat on the sofa holding a tiny ball of fur.

"Happy birthday! Right before you get too excited…."

"I know, I know I'll walk him every day, I promise."

"And you don't get to keep Tom."

"I thought this was a two for one kind of deal."

Tom laughed, handing Alex the small puppy who immediately curled up on her lap; closed his eyes and fell asleep; he gave her a wink and a kiss on the cheek and sat back down.

"The breeder told us that out of all his siblings, none have grown to be above two kilos. They are very small and probably won't grow any more than a handful."

"He's so cute he can stay this size forever!" she said giddily with excitement.

"What's his name?" she asked, running her hand along his soft white fur.

"He doesn't have one; it's up to you."

"Really?"

"One hundred per cent."

Alex took a long look at the sleeping pup; run her hand through his fur and took a moment to think.

"Fabdog."

"Try again," Tom chuckled.

"I like Ollie." she smiled.

"I really like that. Right, now the last surprise."

"Whilst I've been in here, distracting you with a puppy; John has ordered pizza and he should have..."

"Space fight? Really?" John asked confused walking into the room holding the DVD to show Alex.

"No way?"

This sounds like a rip-off, right?"

"Oh, it is in every sense of the word; Tom are you staying to watch this?"

"Yeah, if that's okay with John?"

"Of course; I already ordered food for you bud."

"Sweet. I guess we should open these then?" Tom said, reaching down the side of the sofa and pulling out a crate of Whitfield's.

He cracked one open; handed it straight to John before opening another and taking a sip.

"Ahem!" Alex exclaimed loudly.

Tom stopped mid-sip and handed the beer to Alex; she smiled, blew him a kiss and took a sip.

As the night drew to a close and the sun went down, John looked across the sofa to see Alex had fallen asleep on Tom; her head rested on his lap and Ollie sat nestled in between the two of them.

"Pst!" John ushered towards Tom.

Tom looked over at John.

"Do you want me to move her?" He asked quietly.

"You're alright; she's completely gone. Go on get yourself to bed, I'll sort this one out."

"You sure mate?"

"Yeah, you've been running around all day, go on get some rest."

Before he went up the stairs, John looked back one last time. He looked at Alex, who had fallen asleep with a large smile spread across her face.

At this moment; nothing else mattered...she was happy.

Alex giggled looking up at Tom. They locked eyes as he ran a hand through her hair, looking deeply into her bright green eyes nothing was said.

She closed her eyes as their fingers intertwined.

Initial Enquiries

John laid unconscious...his face half sunk in a puddle of blood that had seeped from the back of his head and nose. Ollie sat next to him nudging him and whining loudly trying to get his attention.

He rolled onto his back and sat forward pain shooting through his entire body as he sat up and grabbed the back of his head trying to see how bad the damage was.

He reached a little higher and upon feeling the bone protruding from his skull, he shot forward and hurled into his lap spitting sick and blood. John rolled forward; slapped his bloodied hand on the floor and tried to stand, it was so slippery it took a few attempts.

He pulled himself up and stumbled to the kitchen.

Leaving bloodied handprints along the way, John dragged himself through the kitchen. He swung open the door and made his way to the sink. He ran cold water onto his head and washed the blood off; before wrapping it tightly in bandages. He used glue to stick together the rest of the open wounds that now covered his face, from split lips to a large slit that ran along his nose.

He took Ollie upstairs; filled a bath with warm water and washed him before checking for any cuts or scrapes.

Ollie was fine. He'd fought viciously and had come out lucky.

"Good boy," John said stroking him gently and checking his fur in the process.

Before taking himself downstairs and cleaning the blood that had puddled on a spot in front of the back door.

John walked towards the back door and looked out at the long concrete path that led down to a small patch of grass. The sun, now rising, left a golden bed of light along the garden that made the amount of blood John had lost visible.

He caught a glimpse of his reflection in the glass door and was taken aback. Looking into his now fully red eyes. The bloodshot had spread like a virus, covering the green in his eyes like a blanket.

The veins now covered his entire neck leaving a feeling like hands gripped tight; leaving every breath as painful as the last.

As his vision blurred and his sight began to fade, John looked up to see the figure now stood at the edge of the pathway.

He paced as a man possessed; full of rage and hatred.

He turned and made his way for the door stopping just before the glass; his chest-beating heavily.

John looked deep into his eyes, one red, one now green; his face wrapped tightly in clean white bandages and a hood that covered the majority of his head.

"I'm not scared of you," John screamed - his voice now hoarse.

The figure remained unfazed; his chest still beating heavy as he raised a hand and ran his fingers along the window.

"I said I'm not scared of you," he took a step back, grabbed the curtains and closed them. He dropped to a knee as the pain shot through his body like adrenaline.

He turned and looked around the room before grabbing the dining table and dragging it in front of the door; he piled the units up high blocking out the remaining light.

'The police,' John thought. He ran to the front door and swung it open before coming face to face with an officer who had a hand raised just about to knock.

"What happened to you?" the officer asked sternly; lowering his hand.

"It was..." John looked up at the officer staring back at him; over his shoulder stood the hooded figure.

He looked into John's eyes as he moved closer to the officer who waited patiently unaware of the devil on his back.

The figure stood behind the officer closely; close enough that he should have felt his breath on his neck - but the officer remained unfazed.

"Sir...Are you okay?" he asked, concern in his voice.

"I, uh, I fell. Think I drank too much. I'm fine...is everything okay?"

"I'm here to ask about Mr Cairn, you mind if I come in?"

"Uhh, yeah sure," John moved aside to let the officer pass through as the figure moved towards John, he took a step inward and froze.

The figure stopped at the foot of the door and stared at John; enraged his chest-beating heavy.

John looked down at the foot of the door; looked back up at him and smiled.

The officer walked through peeking through the hallway, noticing very quickly the path of destruction through the house.

"I need to ask - where were you yesterday when Mr Cairn was attacked? Did you and he have a close relationship? I know there was friction between the two of you?"

"I'm guessing you didn't question the rest of the people on this road?"

"I did actually," The officer scoffed. "Not much of it I can use though. He really wasn't popular huh?"

"Pretty much; he spent the majority of his free time pissing off people and trying his hardest to make sure people did not like him."

"Why would he do that?" the officer asked inquisitively.

"You tell me."

"We've got officers searching his house now. Hopefully, that will give us some clue on who he was."

"I was actually with a couple of friends last night. I can give you their contact details if you need them."

"Please."

John took a pen and pad from the officer and began writing Tom's name and number.

"His name is Tom Gordon, we work to…"

"The Journalist?"

"Yeah. You know him?"

"Yeah; small world," the officer chuckled.

"I'll give him a call and get back to you. Thank you for your time," The officer tore off a note and handed it to John.

"My number - if you think of anything else," the officer looked John up and down intently.

"Do you want me to send over a medic? Get someone to have a look at your head?"

"I'm honestly fine, thank you."

"Appreciate it," the officer stood up, shook John by the hand and left.

John shut the door, locked everything that could be locked, turned around and climbed up the stairs slowly; every step feeling the bruising on his hands and feet dull and painful. Turning left at the top of the staircase, he walked into Alex's room.

Opening the door, Ollie ran straight past him and Jumped up onto her bed, curling in a ball at the end.

"I'm sorry bud, I miss her too,"

He sat on the foot of the bed and ran his hands through Ollie's fur.

John looked at the bedside cabinet that sat dusty, filled with photos, old photographs... memories.

He reached over and grabbed the closest one; dusted it off and took a look.

The photo was of John and Alex, at a convention; dressed in outfits that even after all these years John still wasn't sure who they were.

He'd remembered how excited she was bringing the costumes back and scoffed at how stressful he'd remember the day being - from the tickets that sold out within minutes to the lines that seemed to go on forever; although when they'd spoken about it all she remembered was the laughing.

They had chuckled and scoffed in jest at some of the craziest parts of the day; the great costumes and those that took it far too seriously; remaining in character throughout the day.

He smiled putting the photo back before picking up another. The photo was Alex and Tom. She smiled for the camera as he looked at her laughing. He had no idea when this was taken but seeing her like this made him smile.

Before putting the photo down John noticed a packet of cigarettes, half full, hidden at the back on the unit.

"Cheeky," he laughed, pulling one out and lighting it. He took a long drag feeling the burn in his throat and closing his eyes through enjoyment before putting the photo back where he found it.

John winced pulling himself up to his feet and walking downstairs. He walked through to the dining room; grabbed the table and pulled it back.

He pulled the curtains open but the garden was clear.

"Where are you! Come on I know you're out there!"

"Come out."

The garden appeared empty. The sky, a bland shade of grey leaving everything underneath it feeling lifeless and dull.

John ran to the kitchen, pulled open a drawer and grabbed a rolling pin before walking back unlatching the back door and stepping out.

"I know you're there!" he shouted stepping out barefoot onto the wet floor. Gripping the wooden pin tightly John walked sheepishly into the unknown, feeling the cold winter air hitting his back.

"Are you scared?"

John waved the rolling pin wildly, screaming into the void.

"That's what I thought! You cowardly fu...." - the winter chill stopped as a warm breath hit John's neck.

Christmas Bliss

Alex sat smiling in her chair, steaming hot coffee in front of her as she flicked through comics humming to herself quietly. Ollie sat at her feet, large and fluffy. He followed her all over the house, like a cloud drifting where every attention could be found; often at Alex's feet if not by her side. He rarely strayed.

"Buddy," she called out, ripping a streak of bacon from the table and passing it down to him; the only thing that could bring him from his slumber. He raised his head took the bacon gently and immediately put his head back down.

Taking a sip of coffee, she pulled out her phone; held it outstretched before taking a picture.

"Enjoy that?" she said pouting at the camera with a goofy smile and a wink.

"What are you up to?" John laughed, coming through the kitchen.

"Uh, nothing! shut up," she replied putting her phone down before it buzzed quietly on the table.

"Someone's keen."

"Who?"

"Whoever replied almost instantly."

"Shut up," she laughed dismissively.

"I'm a grown-ass woman and I can't help it that I look like this."

"I'm gonna ignore that," he said; sitting down coffee in hand, reaching over for the Gazette placed in the middle of the table.

"Hey John, I've been meaning to talk to you about something," holding a hand over her screen as it buzzed again.

"Is it about that?"

"No," she laughed.

'That's for another day,' She thought to herself.

"I want to get back to work."

"Work? like a job?"

"Like a job," she smiled.

"I've been thinking about it and I want to get back out! I miss working. I miss being out in the world, being a part of something. You know I've felt so useless having to rely on this chair and I have found someone willing to take me on."

"Okay...anyone I know."

"Actually, yes...umm Tom agreed to take me on."

"Tom...my Tom? Tom, Tom?"

"Yeah, that one. And before you say anything I'll be in an office and he's promised wheelchair access."

"Okay if you think you're ready, but you know that makes me your boss."

"I'm gonna regret this aren't I?"

"No, I'm a strict but fair ruler," he said, laughing to himself.

"So, when do you think you'll start?"

"Monday," she smiled.

"Monda-" John spat out his coffee and laughed.

"Right, yeah cool cool cool."

"Is that okay?"

"Of course. Yeah, I'm glad if you think you're ready, then that's good. So, you'll be paying for your own comics from now on then?"

She said nothing; just lifted her warm coffee and brought it to her lips.

The months that followed went in a blur. Alex took to working alongside John like she'd been there forever. She was hard working and there wasn't a co-worker that had a bad word to say about her.

By the end of the year, Alex had progressed well within the company. Her easy-going personality had made her a wonder to work with and much beloved.

"I can't believe it's a been a year," Alex whispered, excitement in her voice.

They stood in the middle of the office Christmas party, drinks in hand; enjoying the festivities, people were walking by and greeting Alex and John.

"You are amazing," Maude said, walking past and whispering something in Alex's ear.

"What was that about?" John asked.

"Haha, I'll tell you later," She chuckled.

"Johnny...Can I steal you please?" Maude asked, directing John away.

"Of course."

Maude stood at around five foot nine with long dark hair, cherry red lips, and deep brown eyes. She wore a long tight-fitting yellow dress and had a dark complexion that was absent a single blemish.

"I wanted to thank you, Johnny," she said, ushering John out onto the balcony usually reserved for smoke breaks; she handed John a whiskey and reached into her pocket and pulled out a cigar.

"Thank me for what?" he said taking one from her and lighting it.

"Thank you," he smiled.

"For not telling anyone about my ...you know."

"Girlfriend? Don't worry about that. I wouldn't say anything, I got you."

"You're not a big of a dick as people say you know," she laughed lighting her cigar and nudging her shoulder against his.

A soft blanket of snow fell as they stood on the cold balcony watching the cars go by in the distance and the occasional firework that shot up lighting the night's sky.

Wakefield in the winter was beautiful with its unique combination of modern and historical architecture lit up like a Christmas tree. The entire city came together in unison every year to make sure every street light and window was adorned with tinsel and lights, leaving a feeling of magic in the air

Often described almost like a neon steampunk wonderland, photographers would come from all over the world to view the city - all trying to take the perfect photograph; each trying to capture moments of tranquillity and euphoria along the streets.

"Alex, pst," she turned around to see Tom standing behind her dressed in a red Christmas blazer complete with matching tie and reindeer antlers, holding two drinks.

"You look...nice," she winced smiling.

"I lost a bet... come on I want to show you something," he gently eased his way through the crowd, always looking back to make sure Alex was close enough.

He led Alex past all the people, often stopping to shake hands and say hello on his way through. Passing underneath some mistletoe in a doorway, he stopped and gave her a wink.

"You wish," she laughed pushing him forward.

"Where are we going?" she giggled.

"Right here," he said, opening a door.

"This is your new office...um if you want it."

"What?" she replied, shocked.

"Well, you've been amazing. I mean you've been really great and don't tell your brother, but I prefer working with you... fewer bouts of rage. You've been so great that in the new year, this will be your new office."

"Oh my god! thank you."

"Oh, don't thank me. I tried claiming this office for myself but they were having none of it!"

"Asshole," she laughed, slapping him playfully.

"And there's a couple more things," Tom went behind the desk and pulled out a wrapped box about two-foot square.

Smiling, she unwrapped it; resting the box on her lap.

"It's a..."

"Mini fridge."

"Yeah, it made more sense in my fridge."

"Fridge?"

"Head. It made more sense in my head," he corrected himself.

"No, it's perfect," she smiled.

"Where should I put it?"

"I think..." he took the fridge and plugged it in on the left side of the desk.

"There, now you never have to travel far."

"Thank you!" she smiled gleefully.

"So, what's the other present?"

Tom took the wrapping paper; balled it up and threw it in the bin before reaching behind the desk and pulling out a small vine of mistletoe.

Alex raised an eyebrow and smiled.

Victor Reardon

The Unwelcome Visitor

John stood alone frozen by fear; his socks soaking up every ounce of wet and cold, leaving his feet numb as the cold air attacked the rest of his body.

Feeling a warm breath on his neck, he felt almost paralyzed. His chest sunk ever deeper into an abyss as he desperately searched for a way out.

Feelings of guilt, embarrassment and anxiety filled his chest like water in his lungs, making every breath more difficult than the last; although it was hard at this point to tell the difference between the physical and mental pain. Merely standing up felt like a battle but he had to endure - this wasn't the end.

"What do you want?" he turned to look at the looming presence that stood behind him, whose eyes had now both turned a bright shade of green; his face still wrapped tightly in bandages.

The figure stood aggressively, his chest-beating like a warrior after a battle. He seethed anger and resentment, yet he stood still; patient like an animal ready to strike at any moment.

"Come on!" John said, pushing the figure who barely moved.

"I said come on!" he screamed. His voice echoing in the distance as he pushed the figure once more, this time harder.

The figure stepped a foot back and instantly cracked John back, hitting him hard enough to send him falling onto his backside. John climbed back onto his feet, grunting painfully in the process.

"That all you got?" John taunted, wiping blood off his chin and throwing a punch back, in vain. The figure stepped back and cracked John on the back of his head causing the wound to open up, spraying blood down his back.

The night was silent as darkness crept up on John. The garden now lit only by the moon. He fought viciously, the figure never stopping and never tiring. Blood pooled on the floor around them as John dropped to his knees. His eyes were black and a sharp bone protruded from his nose that had now gone past the point of broken. John's lungs crackled with every breath, forcing him to spit blood back up.

He coughed a glob of blood onto the floor. John stood back up his lungs wheezed.

The figure walked slowly towards him. He reached his hands out, trying to keep the figure from getting too close.

"I'm done!" he rasped; the figure still creeping forward.

"Please!"

The figure pushed onward; knocking Johns arms out of the way and grabbing his throat; pushing hard with its thumbs on John's Adam's apple; squeezing tightly.

Trying to fight it; John tried desperately to push the figure away.

"Please!" he cried again.

All of a sudden, the figure stopped, stood high and took a step back. John scrambled to his feet and made for the door not looking back. He threw himself through the doorway smashing into a unit on the way through.

He turned and slammed the door shut.

Breathing heavily, John fell onto his back and scrambled desperately to come back to reality.

"Why are you doing this?" he cried.

"I can't do it!"

For what seemed like a lifetime, John laid on the empty cold floor, his chest beating hard as anxiety weighed heavy. His heart sunk as it filled with guilt and regret.

His sobbing turned to laughter as the pain increased and the hole in his chest became deeper and deeper. He curled up into a ball, gripping his legs tightly and falling onto his side. He just laid there staring at the floor...waiting for the pain to end.

John awoke to the sun coming up, beaming through the hole's in the curtains onto his face as Ollie pawed at him.

"I'm alive...please don't eat me," he laughed painfully, pushing himself back up onto his feet.

Taking himself upstairs John stared into the mirror looking at the bone sticking out of his nose.

"No, no, no, no, no," he said grabbing his nose with his index finger and his thumb and attempting to push the bone back in.

"Arrrrgghhhhhh, no!" he screamed, the pain shooting violently through his head, causing him to spit up blood and vomit into the sink.

Looking back at his nose, he could see the bone still poking out. He opened the medicine cabinet on the other side of the mirror and grabbed a mouthguard.

He bit down on it as hard as he could. Clenching tightly and with a hard grip using his thumb, he pushed hard and fast on the bone. Bolts of pain, like lightning, shot through his head forcing him to spit the mouthguard into the sink followed by bloodied sick.

He looked up into the mirror. His eyes were now almost all red; indistinguishable from what was eye and what was bloodshot. His veins now luminous, covered the majority of his face.

Blood spilt into the sink sequentially like a heart beating, a ticking clock counting down. He wrapped the top of his head tightly with a bandage to stem the bleeding and some attempt at keeping the skin from peeling off his skull.

A pitted feeling of sick knotted in John's stomach. He retched over the sink before splashing cold water onto his face and swishing some of it around his mouth.

"Come on boy," John called out. "Buddy? where are you?"

He walked out of his bedroom to no response. Looking down the vacant hallway he noticed the door of Alex's room ajar.

He crept down the hallway, pacing silently. Every step hurting like needles running up his legs.

He gently pushed the door inwards to see Ollie laid on Alex's bed asleep and breathing gently.

He'd never know what happened to that smiling, green-eyed, innocent face that he had grown up with, that had fed him, bathed him. That had always been a part of his pack but he'd certainly noticed her absence.

John didn't say a word as he crept in, gave Ollie a gentle stroke checking his fur in the process; stole the now half-empty pack of cigarettes and crept back out, leaving the door open partially to allow some light in.

Walking back into his room John grabbed his phone that still sat on his bedside table and went to check his messages. Dead battery. He put it on charge, walked into the ensuite and began drawing himself a bath.

Running no hot water; John laid in the ice-cold bath feeling every pain and ache numb with the cold water. He lit a smoke and laid there bare, soaking...numb....broken.

John's phone turned on with the charge and begun going crazy. He pulled himself out of the bath, dabbed himself off with a towel and put it back. Walking into the bedroom, he grabbed the phone and begun searching through it.

Maude - seven messages unread 'call me, where are you' etc.

Tom - sixteen unread messages.

'Call me.'

'Need to talk.'

'Where the fuck are you?'

John dialled his number and called him.

"Dude where the fuck have you been? I've been trying to get a hold of you. Is everything ok?"

"Yeah, I've been busy. I'm sorry mate."

"Right; too busy for your job? Boss is pissed. I've told him you're on assignment. There's only so much I can cover for you."

"I know, dude, I know. I just need a few days. I haven't been feeling very well."

"Right. Well in future, you call that shit in."

"I know, I know. I'm sorry, dude"

"It's alright as long as you're okay. That's all that matters. look shut up for a second. Are you safe?"

"Safe? Yeah, I'm fine. I've been at home ill for a few days but I'm good."

"Okay. Just know I've got your back," Tom said, looking down at a pile of now dark red photographs taken from the interview with Mrs Celeste. Most taken inside were very normal, but one that stood out shook Tom to his core. Standing on the patio, notebook in hand, John stood there waiting for Celeste to open the door, but something was behind him - lurking.

"I appreciate it man; have you heard anything on Heath?"

"I'm waiting for a call. They've been searching his house. My guy's been in contact but he's been MIA for a couple of days. Must have been important, whatever he found. We'll know soon."

"Talk soon...love you, bro."

"And you."

Days began passing in a blur as his anxiety increased. John realised there was no longer an outside, not one for him anyway.

Barricading the windows and doors John hid away. He would often awake in the early hours of the morning and the dead silence. If he listened closely, he could hear the figure stirring in the darkness; stewing in rage and hatred it paced relentlessly outside the house.

Eventually, he began drowning the noise out with music; quiet at first but each night it got a little louder. There was only so long he could avoid work. He thought about running to and from his car each day, which was ridiculous. The only saving grace was that in today's day and age he could do all his food shopping online but then would be endangering the delivery driver? There wasn't an instruction manual for this.

The only thing he had known at this point was that the figure couldn't get inside. Mrs Celeste must have known this to run to the other side of the planet and hide away for most of her life.

Another night alone, John wandered through the house aimlessly as he clutched another half-empty bottle of whiskey. His head spun and the world around him turned. John would often stand looking outside the upstairs window; watching the world slowly move on without him. He thought about how he would live like this. How long until the figure that had pursued him relentlessly stopped, would he get bored? Would it wait until John grew old and died? Time sped so fast he feared it wouldn't be long until he found out.

Star Wars & Pizza

"I don't understand," John asked sitting forward and grabbing a slice of steaming hot pizza; the smell of warm cheese filling the air.

"What's not to understand?" Alex responded, sitting across the room.

"Right, well this is set, what, 18 years after the last one?"

"17, yeah."

"Right and how has Obi Ben Kenobi aged so much in that time?"

"I think you're overthinking it," Alex laughed "People aged a lot different back then. It could be something to do with the two suns constantly bearing down on him. I mean how no one on this planet is fried like bacon I'll never know."

"Okay, okay, okay, another thing."

"Go on."

"She's a princess, right?"

"Yep."

"Well after her planet got destroyed, they still call her it; as well as how rich she is?"

"Did she not keep her money in a bank on her own planet?"

"I actually can't answer that one."

"Right last question, I swear. Why is Luke more upset that the space wizard dies than his aunt and uncle getting barbequed not an hour before?"

"What's your goal here?" Alex laughed, grabbing a beer and twisting the top off.

"I'm genuinely just curious. It's actually alright. I'm not joking I like this; I love the hairy bear dude."

"Okay that's Chewbacca, and you put some respect on his name," She said clicking her fingers at John.

"Shall we start questioning what you like?"

"Bring it on. You've got nothing."

"Chalet Girl, Confessions of a shopaholic?"

"Really? you're a grown-ass man!"

"I stand by both of those as great movies!"

"Yeah, that's what I thought!" Alex laughed pulling her wheelchair closer and lifting herself into it stopping John before he went to stand up to help.

"I'm good. I got this," she said slipping into her chair.

"You sure?"

"Yeah, thanks bro." she replied rolling herself out the door; "I'll be back."

"Yo, Wheels, bring me back a beer will ya?" he laughed, finishing his drink and threw it into a bin on the side of his sofa.

"Buddy?" John stood up to try and call Alex, when all of a sudden, a thunderous crash echoed through the house.

He ran out into the kitchen to see Alex lying face down; her chair knocked over - wheels still spinning.

Her eyes had rolled into the back of her head and she was convulsing aggressively on the floor.

"Alex!" He screamed running over, panic filling his body. John rolled her onto her right side and placed one of her arms under her head to keep it propped up.

"Alex, can you hear me? Can you hear anything I'm saying?" he put two fingers on her neck and kept them there; feeling for a pulse. "I'm calling an ambulance! everything's gonna be alright, just stay with me! please stay with me."

"It would appear your sister's condition has worsened and we're gonna need to keep an eye on her. I do have to ask, you're her brother, right? Are you in contact with your parents at all? I've got no details for them on file?" Whispered the doctor quietly after pulling John to the side of the room discreetly.

"I'm sorry we haven't spoken since she was diagnosed. The whole thing was a bit much for them and they went out one night and never came back."

"I'm sorry to hear that. Shall I put you down as primary carer?"

"Yeah of course."

"We are going to monitor her condition, Mr Mason, and see which way to proceed."

"John's fine. thank you, doc," John pulled up a chair and sat next to Alex, who hadn't woken up since passing out.

"I'm sorry it took so long. I got stuck in traffic." Tom said, bursting through the door; "How is she?" he asked, his voice breaking.

"It's too early to tell. All they can do is monitor her and hope for the best."

"Got these from the machine from outside," Tom said, handing John a coffee and sitting down beside him.

"Thanks for coming mate, I really appreciate it."

John sat back, coffee warming his hands staring at Alex who still hadn't woken up. She lay peacefully; eyes closed, unaware of what was happening around her.

"You know I tried calling my mum? I thought she ought to know what's been going on," John scoffed.

"She changed her number...can you believe that? I've been in here pacing this fucking room."

John said trying desperately to hold back his tears "What kind of parent would fucking do that?"

"I was thinking about the night they left, you know? She was 14! Since that night she's never mentioned it or asked about them. We've got no pictures of them in the house."

"What kind of person just gets to decide that it's no longer their fucking responsibility? You know?" John paused...He sat there staring at Alex, still unmoved as he tried desperately not to cry. His eyes welling up, but he wouldn't ever let himself cry not over them.

His chest pounded as guilt weighed like an anvil, heavy on his chest.

"She's always been so strong."

John stood up and turned around. He looked out at the window and stared at all the people in the distance going about their daily lives.

"I wish we could trade places. I just wish there was something I could do?"

"You're here for her, that's all that matters now and that's the best we can do," Tom looked up. He could see John sobbing quietly, trying not to make a noise. He stood up and made his way across the room, grabbed John and hugged him tightly.

For a moment neither men said a thing.

"Ughh, huhh," John cleared his throat. "I'm going to go grab a tissue; you alright to watch her for a moment?"

"Course, mate."

John left. Tom took a moment watching Alex as she lay sleeping peacefully. He reached into his pocket, pulled out a small box and clutched it in his hand tightly.

He kissed her gently on the forehead and slipped the box back into his pocket; saying nothing.

The Secret Room

It was the dead of night there wasn't a sound in the distance apart from the rare car passing by or pisshead still trying to find their way home long after closing time. The police had packed up and gone home. The only remains were that of police tape and a single officer left on guard duty.

No one had ever turned up for heath; no family or friends had come to check on him. They had begun bagging his belongings and throwing them out onto the street. John watched from a slit between his curtains; looking down in the street. The hooded figure stood looking up at him waiting patiently.

John closed the curtains and made his way back through the house; now having to rely on Alex's cane, something had clicked in his left knee and nothing he did could get it to go back. He sealed the wound on the back of his head closed with glue though difficult to see, it throbbed aggressively.

He stood alone in his kitchen; naked, the only things he wore were blood-stained bandages and a half-smoked cigarette as his temperature burned hot like a wildfire spreading all over.

He'd blocked the windows and doors with furniture and units from around the house. Nothing was getting in he'd thought to himself. Although the figure made no effort to try; it was better to be safe.

John's mind raced with questions. Why could no one else see this thing? could it be hurt?

He'd fought it tooth and nail, but then again, he was never much of fighter. He'd only stayed at the boxing club in his youth because of the coach's daughter. It made being punched every Wednesday and Saturday worth it.

The cupboards were almost bare, save for some dog food. *'I'm not that hungry,'* he'd thought to himself, doubling over as each chuckle had felt like a new punch to his rapidly thinning waistline.

Looking around at the destruction he'd caused, John began scrambling through items thrown across the floor, grabbing books, anything that he thought would help. A half-finished bottle of whiskey in hand and a cigarette in the other - there he sat, drinking and smoking alone, feeling the nicotine burn his throat as anxiety ripped his body apart like cancer overwhelming his body.

At this point, it was hard to tell what was causing the dizziness. It could be the infection coming from the head wound held together by glue or the whiskey coursing through his veins.

John sat cross-legged watching out the back door window at the creature pacing back and forth.

It turned to look at John, still pacing aggressively kicking rain with every step. The patio had stained red with blood. It stopped abruptly and begun walking towards John, keeping eye contact with him the whole time.

Remaining seated, too tired to move, John looked up watching the figure.

The figure looked down on him for a moment before sitting down and crossing its legs. Staring deep into John's eye's he said nothing.

***

"Officer Clement?"

"Yes Sir," He said sternly, standing straight arms crossed behind his back.

"Have you found anything yet?"

"Nothing so far. I've interviewed almost everyone on this road and they've all said roughly the same thing."

"And that is?"

"That he was a dickhead...sir, that's a direct quote from the eighty-one-year-old lady with the Zimmer frame next door. Apparently, a month back, he'd refused to make way for wheelchair access for her and then screamed at her, causing her to cry in front of her three grandchildren."

"Dickhead," the officer scoffed.

"Yes sir."

"Officer Clement?"

"Yes sir?"

"At ease, you can relax. You're not serving the military anymore."

"Sorry, sir; force of habit."

"I understand and no 'sir' come on; Dan's fine. I'm you're superior in position only, you can relax. What else have we got?"

"Officer Jones smelled heavy bleach in Mr Cairns car, so we've had it sent off for forensic testing. Of all the people we interviewed the one that stood out to me was a Mr..." he said, pulling out a small notepad from his breast pocket and scrolling quickly. "....Mason. When officer Jones spoke to him, the first time he was pissed but by all accounts, all seemed normal. But when he says he went back in the morning, he looked like he'd taken a beating. I spoke to some neighbours who said they'd never got along but that by all accounts other than some heavy drinking everyone seems to like Mr Mason."

"Alcoholic?"

"Functioning Alcoholic, but his alibi is solid, sir. Other than Mr Cairn being unpleasant as a neighbour, there seems to be no real motive."

"And where is Jones now?"

"Still searching the house."

"Good work officer."

"Thank you, sir...Dan."

Officer Clement waited patiently. Composed like a soldier, he stood at around six foot three with a large muscular frame and short shaved black hair, dark skin and bright blue eyes. To his fellow officers, he was often spoken about in hushed tones.

Not much was known about him but they all had stories or had heard rumours. Some were clearly exaggerated. One consistent thing, he had been a good soldier and there was always a sense you were going to be safe when he was around.

One story that was often told, was that of his first day the officer. He'd been shadowing and gave chase to a suspected group of thieves. By the time he had caught up, his superior was lying face down on the ground and they'd taken his gun and nightstick. He was bleeding profusely on the floor. When the officer came round; Officer Clement had disarmed the men and arrested all three before tending to his wounds, possibly saving his life.

This story had been told and retold a thousand times throughout the precinct. But for him it was part of the job as well as being infinitely safer than serving in the armed forces; something he'd loved doing in his youth but once his daughter was born was no longer an option.

He'd stood there when she was born, holding her in his arms, and he'd known at that moment that it was time to come home for good.

"Hey, Clement," Officer Jones called out.

"Clement, get in here."

Turning around and walking in, Officer Clement immediately turned on the torch attached to his chest and put on the blue rubber gloves he'd had in his back pocket so as to not contaminate the crime scene.

The house was dark. It would appear at some point in the dead of night, the power had gone out and no one had been able to get it back on. The house was bare, save for a small TV and sofa in the living room and not much food in the kitchen.

"Hey, Clement, answer me something."

"Yeah, go on."

"There's fuck all here, right?"

"Seems like that, yeah."

"Okay, so help me out, because there is something I don't understand," Said the officer walking up and shutting the door behind officer Clement.

"Look at this."

The door had three thick locks, one right at the top, a bolt at the bottom and in the middle a large circular lock that looked too big for the door.

"Guy must have valued his privacy, right?"

"It's more than that though. It's the same on every door. Check this out."

He led Clement through the house and he was right; every room the same.

"But there's fuck all here? I mean, even if someone made it past all those locks, there isn't anything for them to take right?"

"Unless he was trying to keep something from leaving," Officer clement suggested, looking past Jones' shoulder.

"You feel that breeze?"

"Yeah?"

"It's coming from there," he said, moving past Officer Jones and making his way towards a large empty bookshelf pushed up into the darkest corner of Heath's house.

"Help me with this," he asked, grabbing the side and pulling it towards him.

Pulling the bookcase across the wall revealed a large tunnel that from the outside appeared endless.

"What the fuck?"

Officer Clement preceded slowly down it, unholstering his police-issue Glock 17 and treading carefully through the hole.

The tunnel spiralled round and led directly under the house. Cold, damp and dark they followed it. He gripped the gun tightly, taking the safety off and pulling the hammer back.

Officer Jones followed closely behind; keeping his left hand on Clement's right shoulder the entire time.

"Careful" He warned, stepping down out of the tunnel. The room was small but packed with junk; from old half-soaked unlabelled boxes and tools scattered haphazardly around.

"Check those; I'll keep going," he said quietly moving gently forward.

Officer Jones pulled down a box from the top of a stack and begun looking through it. Old photos, at first glance what appeared to be pictures taken at a party; the next taken of a young child smiling in a park.

'They told me he had no family,' he thought to himself.

Another photo, the same girl this time alone and she wasn't smiling; she was crying...

"Oh no," he said scrolling through.

Jones pulled out another picture, he lifted his torch to it to get a better look and without saying anything, he dropped it and ran to the side of the room retching and throwing up.

His whole body shook as he put a hand on the wall in front of him and breathed deeply, trying to regain some sort of composure. He looked at his hands, they were shaking. He clenched his fists and took another deep breath before standing up straight and wiping the tears from his eyes.

"Shit! Clement!" he called out as he moved slowly past the boxes. "Where are you?" he turned the corner to see the officer his on his knees.

"It's going to be okay," he was repeating calmy.

"Fuck!" he exclaimed to himself, noticing Officer Clement was clutching something close to him...

Jones moved closer, slowly realising that Officer Clement was holding a small child close him and she was sobbing quietly into his chest.

"Call this in."

"I've got you,".

He turned and ran back up the tunnel. Officer Clement held the child tightly, trying to calm her down. She'd clearly been down there a while. Her clothes were wet and frayed. Her lips were blue and her eyes were a shade of black. It was obvious she had been hit. Looking closely under the bruising was a soft shaded fade of blue.

Officer Clement took off his grey jacket and wrapped it around the young girl tightly. Her shivering slowly calmed as she watched him intently.

"Come on," he said, taking her hand and turning towards the door. Before he could move, she began shaking again. She refused to move any further.

"Oh hey, hey, it's okay."

"No one's gonna hurt you. I've got you."

He could see the fear in her eyes as she looked at the doorway; her lips trembling uncontrollably.

"Come here," he said, dropping to his knee and reaching his arms out, without saying a word or wasting a second, the girl climbed into his arms.

Resting her forehead on his shoulder, she sobbed quietly as she was carried through the house; never looking up. When the light from the streetlights hit her, she tucked her head in further.

It was clearly the first time she'd seen light in a long time.

Holding her closely, he opened the backdoor to his squad car, but as he tried putting her in, she gripped tighter and tighter refusing to let go.

"It's okay; I've got you," he said gently, closing the door and leaning against a wall.

He couldn't imagine the horrors she'd faced, but he knew at this moment that she was scared and if he could relate to anything, it was being a scared child. He'd spent enough of his own childhood alone in the dark.

"Ambulance is called and backup's on the way," Jones announced sitting down next to Clement. "She okay?" he asked, looking over to see the little girl still hadn't let go her fists clenched tightly holding on.

"No...but she's safe."

As the sun rose that morning, Officer Clement sat patiently in the waiting room of the emergency unit, watching doctors and nurses running frantically in and out of her room. He clutched a small blue toy dog that he'd brought from the gift shop. It was the last one on the shelves but at the time it seemed like a good idea.

He held it in his hand twisting it and turning it just waiting to be allowed in.

"Officer Clement?"

"How's she getting on?" he asked, standing up to talk to the exhausted nurse as she took off her gloves.

"Physically she's fine...mentally it's gonna take some time. There's no real telling the full extent of what she's been through."

"I can imagine."

"You were the one that found her, right?"

"Yes, I uh, yeah."

"Has anyone checked you over?"

"No, I'm fine. Thank you though. I'm just - I've been sat there thinking about what she must have been through? You know?" he said, taking a breath.

"Honestly...we're still running tests, but I've been doing this long enough to know, you know? It almost broke me seeing that poor girl's hands."

"Her hands?"

"Yeah, blood under her nails and bruising on her knuckles...She'd umm," she said, composing herself and wiping away a tear with the back of her hand. "It means she'd fought like hell," she continued; her voice breaking.

"You can go through if you want. If you need anything, I'll be just outside."

"Thank you," he replied. Slowly opening the door, as soon as he walked in, he could see her laying there. She immediately looked up at him, at first a moment of panic, then calm.

"Hey," he uttered quietly, walking over and sitting down on the seat placed next to her bed. "I erm...got you this," he added handing her the small dog. Without saying anything she just grabbed his hand softly and held it tight.

Neither said a word.

Questions & Answers

Wandering through the house, John went from room to room aimlessly, clutching a nearly finished bottle of whiskey.

He burst into the bathroom, almost falling into the bath into the process, looked into the mirror and roared with laughter looking at his face. The veins now covered his entire head and his eyes were almost all red...they looked almost demonic.

Staring into the mirror, John grabbed the last of the bandages that were on the side and wrapped his entire head, leaving only his mouth and eyes uncovered.

He walked through to his bedroom, grabbed a pair of trousers from a cupboard and slid them on. He tumbled downstairs banging into every unit on the way through. The whiskey had numbed the pain enough that most of the smashing didn't hurt; the rest he drunkenly laughed off.

He walked towards the backdoor and pulled the tables blocking it away, grabbing everything he could and stood in front of the door. The hooded figure walked slowly towards him and looked deep into John's eyes.

John looked through his reflection in the glass at the hooded figure, at this point both almost indistinguishable.

"Hahaaaaaa," John roared at him through the window.

The figure looked at him, deep into his eyes before reaching both hands up towards his hood and pulled it down.

"Wha- what are you doing?"

He then reached up again and begun pulling at the bandages on his face, pulling them slowly to reveal the monster underneath.

"No! It can't be! No, no, NO!" he screamed, before falling backwards and throwing the bottle of whiskey towards the door.

It missed and smashed against the wall sending glass flying to the floor. John scrambled to his feet and ran towards the front door; grabbing his keys on the way through. He swung the door open and made his way to his car, never looking back from the moment he left the house to the second he threw himself onto the front seat.

Looking at the road in his rear-view mirror John could see nothing behind him, just an empty road.

For hours he drove across Wakefield through the beautiful vibrant metropolis to the quieter suburbs; avoiding eye contact with the passers-by staring at him through his open window.

At one point he caught a glimpse of himself in the mirror and almost totalled the car mistaking his reflection for the hooded figure.

"HA!" he screamed, stepping on the accelerator.

John's car came to a grinding halt, almost smashing it into a large dead potted plant in the process, before falling out of the door and falling onto the wet ground. Without stopping to shut the car door he turned and made his way up the familiar Indian sandstone steps.

"Hello!" he screamed, banging on the door.

"I know you're there!"

"Come on! Mrs hill!" John screamed at the top of his lungs, banging and smashing on the large wooden door.

"I'm gonna die out here!"

He fell to his knees as his head went red and begun spinning.

"Wooo!" he exclaimed, before falling; his head bouncing off the hard concrete and passing out.

***

"It hurts so bad," Alex complained, pressing the tubes attached to her wrist. "Why do I even need this?" she laughed, holding up a bunch of the random wires.

"Because the doctor said without it you might die."

"Oh, not important then," she scoffed, using the button attached to her bed to sit up.

"I feel like Vader."

"It'll be fine. Look, you've been allowed home, even if we've got to leave you on charge for a while; your home and that's all that matters."

"Did they give you anything for the pain?" she asked looking around the room. "I want the good stuff"

"Yeah, here you go."

He reaches into the cabinet beside the bed and pulled out a syringe. He uncapped it and smiled like a maniac towards her.

"Absolutely not. That thing isn't coming near me," she laughed.

"Haha, not the first time you've said that."

"Actually, this hurts so bad. Stab me!" she commanded, her body convulsing in pain.

John pressed the needle against her wrist and gently squeezed the pump.

"Ahhh, that's not...oh no, that's good."

she smiled, closing her eyes.

"That better?"

"Much," she said before dozing off quickly and peacefully.

John checked on the wires and tubes attached to Alex again before turning around and quietly backing out of the room. He dimmed the lights and looked back to see Ollie asleep on the floor next to the bed.

"Keep an eye on her, bud, yeah?" he whispered before leaving the room.

The doctors had allowed her to come home after spending months in hospital. She'd felt embarrassed and hated the thought of anyone having to look after her. Having spent so long working, she detested the thought of losing her independence again. Finding out she was allowed home was joyous news until she realised just how restricted she would be. Being bed-bound for most of the day and having to rely on other people left her feeling guilty and useless.

***

"Hey! Hey! Wake up."

John awoke abruptly, his heart racing as he scanned the room.

"Why are you here?" Mrs Celeste stood above him wiping her hands on a blood-stained towel and throwing it onto a pile of other blooded towels. "He fucked you up, right?"

Still confused, John pulled himself up and looked her with vacant eyes, still processing his environment.

"Who- who is he?"

"Difficult cultures throughout the years have given her different names."

"Her?" he questioned, grunting in pain and pulling himself up.

"Her. Some called her Oizys others Miseria or Moros. But in every encounter with her, there's always a been one constant.

"And what's that?"

"Sin. I told you. I tried to warn you; she knows what you did."

"I haven't- no I haven't done anything."

"You are lying."

"Can I beat her?"

"Yes."

Mrs Celeste had pulled John into the house, dressed his wounds properly and then left him to rest. He'd slept for days before awaking in the same familiar room.

The smell of old books and oak was almost overpowering.

"Why did you come back?" she asked, handing him a warm drink and calmly sitting down beside him.

"That thing it- it…. Is this chocolate?" he replied confused taking a sip.

"It's good for shock"

The Growing Storm

John awoke in the middle of the night to sniffling and banging. He pulled himself up out of bed and made his way down the familiar hallway. Before reaching the door, he stopped and listened; he could hear Alex writhing and crying. The pain was getting worse every day now with no end in sight.

"Hey shh, shh. I got you," He said, swinging the door open and grabbing the pain medication from the drawer next to her.

He uncapped the lid, put the needle to her arm and gently pushed the liquid through her veins; stopping when half the syringe was empty.

"I- it's John."

She looked up at him, tears in her eyes. She clenched her teeth hard, biting down and praying that the pain would go. She could barely get a full sentence out through the searing pain.

"It won't go, John. It hurts so bad."

Nothing else was said that night as John tried everything he could do to try and soothe out the pain. First whale music, something he'd seen online; worked for sleep anyway.

Next was a shot of whiskey; that one helped him at least.

***

"I've done my part... you need to leave now." Mrs Celeste said, taking the empty cup from John.

"I'm not leaving until you tell me how I can beat this thing! Because right now, I don't see a way out and I'm fucking scared." He said, pulling himself up and standing to face Mrs Celeste.

"What did you do?" she asked sternly, getting so close to John now that their noses almost touched. He took a second as something dawned on him.

"Did you hurt someone? You asked me that the first time we met?" he said, looking around the room; it was spinning now as his mind raced.

John pulled out his phone as he could feel it in his pocket buzzing almost constant.

"John it's Tom, where are you? are you ok? I've been worried sick trying to get a hold of you. Listen I've got an update on Heath."

"Yeah, go on?"

"They found a cellar in his house. Mate, he was fucked up; they found boxes- boxes of uhh…"

"Boxes of what? what did they find?"

"There was stuff. Uhh, kid's stuff; socks, clothes and photos. He hurt a lot of people, John. He was taking these kids from their families. They think whoever killed him was probably a family member of a victim. They found blood residue in his car. He's already been linked to at least thirteen missing kids' cases and here's the thing...they found a girl!"

"Fucking alive in that house? That's why he needed that parking spot, so he didn't have to drag her as far to his fucking car! Fuck man; he fucking deserved what he got. Where are you? We need to talk."

"I'm out. Where are you?"

"I was knocking. You didn't answer, I was worried. I'm in your garden. When are you back?"

"In the gar- Tom you need to get there fuck out of there now!" he screamed.

"Why what's going on listen I'm gonna wait here just get back as soon as you can."

"Fuck! Dead battery," Tom stopped for a moment and looked around - noticing the blood staining the patio in John's garden.

"What the fuh…" it was everywhere; when all of sudden he stopped. The winter's chill had gone but his breath condensed in the cold air. He breathed out again as another cloud of condensation followed. Before he could breathe again, he felt a warm breath...as another cloud fell over his shoulder.

***

John woke once in the middle of the night to sniffling and banging. He could hear crying in the distance.

He pulled himself up out of bed and made his way down the hallway. Before reaching the door, he stopped and listened. He could hear Alex crying; another night in pain.

He gently opened the door and went to the bedside table. Pulling out a syringe, pushing the needle into the veins in her wrist, he gently depressed the plunger down halfway.

As the pain subsided, she lay there, tear's falling down her cheeks.

"I'm sorry John."

"Why are you sorry? Don't be crazy," he said running his hands through her hair and sitting down beside her as she gently drifted off to sleep.

Crime & Retribution

"No, fuck!" he said as the phone died in his hand.

"I killed my husband; not- not that thing."

Mrs Celeste looked at John, her face turning from anger to that of sorrow.

"That night we'd been drinking; drinking heavily..." she paused.

"Oh, he loved a drink; a little too much. And when he drank, he often wanted a little too much...... from me."

"When we met, he was so sweet, gentle and kind. On our first date, he told me he was going to marry me. I introduced him to my mother. She loved him. They don't make 'em like that anymore, she said to me; but on our honeymoon, he changed. He almost damn near killed me for smiling at our waiter too much. The only reason I worked so much was that that was the only time the beatings let up. It would be too hard to get away with being on camera all the time, and that night he'd drank a little too much again. When I refused him for smelling like cigarettes and cheap booze, he put a boot to my face! Said If I didn't give him what he wanted he'd take it. He goes to the kitchen, grabs a knife and holds it up to my throat...laughing while he did it. I was so scared when he grabbed me, I pushed him...he went down and landed on the knife.

"But that wasn't enough to stop him. He said he was going to kill me; I was so scared I grabbed the knife and put it in his chest! Again, and again; I couldn't stop.

"I took his life that night to save my own and that thing- it found me not long after. At first, I couldn't leave my home. I was stuck inside that house before they'd even cleaned up all of my husband's blood.

"I nearly died running here! I ran halfway across the planet to escape that thing and it still found me. It's feeding off your fear and your guilt and it's extremely strong! It's been feeding on me since before you were born.

"You know the worst part of all this? My mum turned eighty this year... I wasn't even there for her. She never understood; how could she? how would I even begin to explain any of this to her?

"I thought I was done, you know? I was going to drink a bottle of whiskey and walk out that front door and just bloody kill myself. I thought before I do that I might as well get some catharsis. That's why I invited you over here...until I saw the way that thing looked at you and for that, I'm so sorry"

John looked at Mrs Celeste. He watched her face the entire time she spoke; she'd never looked at him. The guilt was evident on her face. It had dawned on her how cold she'd become.

She wasn't a killer, before that night she'd never even been in a real fight.

Her voice broke as she finished talking. Before she could say another word, he made his way across the room and grabbed her; wrapped his arms around her and held her tightly. Neither said another word.

Racing home, foot pressed down hard almost constantly on the accelerator; tearing up the road behind him, John held his phone on his lap trying desperately to get a hold of Tom.

"Come on, come on, come on."

"Fuck!" He shouted, bouncing his phone across the car.

John pulled onto his road, the back spinning out and almost smashing into a parked squad car.

"Hey!" A voice called out from across the road. John didn't look back as he burst through his front door tripping on the step. He made his way through the house seeing the carnage he'd caused on the way. The house was turned upside down, units were thrown all over the place; broken glass covered the floor.

Before heading out back, John locked Ollie upstairs to protect him from further harm; still not recovered from the first time they'd run into the hooded figure.

Hurrying into the dining room, John began pulling at the units that covered the back door, sending them tumbling behind him. He pulled open the curtain to see a blood-smeared panel of glass. He took a step back as the figure behind the glass ran its hand slowly down the middle like a bloody curtain opening up to reveal the horrors behind.

There the hooded figure stood, breathing heavily. As it/he/she (John no longer knew how to categories it) pulled away its blooded hand from the window, it moved it forward to show that in its right hand it held Tom by his head. Gripping it tightly by the hair, the apparition ran its fingers across Tom's face, slowly wiping his blood across it.

Tom's eyes opened partially, before closing again - drifting in and out of conciseness. He reached up towards his chest and gripped the green ring attached to his necklace tightly.

John grabbed the key to the back door and turned it slowly. He took a deep breath and stepped out onto the cold, bloody patio.

The figure stepped back, still holding Tom, before throwing him down hard onto the pavement and lifting a hand in John's direction.

"No, wait, wait, wait! Stop!" he yelled, running over to Tom and kneeled beside him.

"I'm so sorry."

"You look like shit," Tom chuckled through bloodied lips as he looked up at john through one open eye; the other swollen over and seeping blood. Tom laughed quietly, his eyes closing again as he winced in pain. His hand still gripping the ring tightly.

The figure stood watching John intently, studying his movements like a game of chess; strategic and calculating.

"Wait, wait, wait! Before you hurt anyone else, I know what you want," he pleaded, raising his hands in the air in surrender and walking towards the figure.

"I know why you followed me...I know what you want; I uhh.." he closed his eyes for a moment and took a deep breath. "I killed her...Alex, it was me. I killed her."

Tom looked up at John through bloodied red eyes as tears stained his cheeks with a look of disgust.

"That's why you followed me right? She was scared and she was in pain. I listened to her crying in agony every night... begging, fucking begging God for the pain to stop."

"And I prayed, I really did, that she'd get better. Every night I prayed, but it wasn't getting better. She was never going to get better, so I made a choice. That's on me; I have to live with that every fucking day." John screamed thumping his hands against his chest.

"I'm fucked, I can barely stand. You've won! look at me."

"I'm ready, so come on! Do your fucking worst. come on!" he screamed. Again, he banged his bruised hands against his chest ready for whatever horrors that were about to come his way."

"Freeze, nobody move!" Officer Clement called out sternly. Bursting through the back door, gun in hand; he raised it to his chest - aiming ahead. In front of him, he saw Tom lying on the floor. Walking to him, he put two fingers under his throat checking his pulse, before continuing forward and standing behind John gun raised.

"Get down on the floor now."

The figure watched John fall to his knees, tears hitting the ground underneath him before turning around and walking away. retreating out the back gate, Officer Clement gave pursuit, but as he turned the corner it was gone.

"Where did he go? who was that?"

John rested on his knees, his face swollen and bruised. As his head spun, he looked back at Tom whose eyes had now closed, saying nothing as he slowly drifted out of consciousness.

Clement walked back towards John, his gun still held tight in his hand.

John held out both hands, wrists pressed together.

"I'm ready."

Officer Clement gripped the walkie talkie attached to his chest and pulled it closer to his mouth before pressing the button.

"I need an ambulance - two men down - suspect escaped on foot - gave chase but he's gone - need a sweep of the area now."

John sat alone. His eyes closed, listening to the commotion around him before the doors to the ambulance swung open.

"How you getting on?" Officer Clement asked calmly, pulling out a notepad and sitting beside him.

"I've been better. How's Tom?"

"He'll be okay. Took a few hard hits but he's tough."

"What happens to me now?"

"That's not up to me."

Epilogue

The airport was manic as people ran back and forth frantically bags in hand; thousands of faces all going different places with a million stories between them.

A young girl ran desperately between people, each one racing in different directions.

She ducked and dodged, keeping an eye on the family ahead of her; the largest member looking back often making sure she was never more than an arm's length out of reach.

At about four foot tall, it was very easy for her to get overwhelmed; especially in large noisy crowds. She tackled it with the bravery of a warrior in battle, constantly on the move, jumping suitcases if she had too.

She carried a backpack; a similar shade of blue to her own eyes. She continued, with a stern look on her face through the zombie-like waves of people, stopping only to stroke the few dogs being led around on leads.

She looked up for a moment, making sure her family was where she left them, before going back and stroking the grey, long-tongued puppy that was being held tightly by its owner. When she looked towards her family, they had disappeared into the crowd.

"Daddy?" She called out, looking around at all the faces; none stopping to notice the small child searching anxiously for her family.

A moment of panic overcame her as the world seemed to almost speed up. She reached into her baggy grey jumper and gripped the toy she'd been carrying in it. When she kept it close to her, she'd always felt safe.

She looked at the people in the crowd again; scanning their faces, their clothes and the way they moved. Seeing a woman with the same hairstyle as her mum and a man with the same pulled up grey hoodie as her dad, she called out.

"Dah-," before she could finish, a set of large hands reached out from the crowd and picked her up, spinning her around and pulled her close.

"Come on. If we don't get to the restaurant before your mum and your sister, you know we won't hear the end of it," the booming voice said, instantly calming her down. She rested her head on his shoulder and watched the world slow down again.

On the other side of the large crowd sat an older lady, happily watching children running around. She marvelled at the world around her, so much different from her youth.

She smiled to herself, keeping a single bag of luggage by her side.

To her the people were beautiful, she'd often put stories the faces in the crowd and smiled at the thoughts.

"Crazy right?" a voice from next to her called out quietly.

"Pardon?"

"How they're born and then the next thing you know, they're just running around causing carnage everywhere they go. I've got two little boys myself...twins," he added, pulling out his wallet and showing a photo. "I'm going home to see them; I hate leaving them, you know?" he said putting the wallet back into his breast pocket. "Sorry it's just clicked," he scoffed. "Crazy person talking about himself at the airport. I'm Sean," he said reaching out his hand.

"Faith," she replied, smiling and shaking it.

"Are you going anywhere nice, faith?"

"Home...I'm going home," she smiled.

The End.

If you have made it to this point, I am eternally grateful that you invested your time in my book.

Thank you

Victor Reardon

About the Author

Victor Reardon grew up in and around the Medway area of Southeast England.

Always an outsider, he found escapism as a child through sports, movies and comic books.

Being a lover of writing, he has recently appeared on a blog page for movie reviews, quickly gaining just under a thousand followers; although a modest number, having that many readers interested in his opinions seems insane to him.

Having a creative mind, he decided to test himself and turn his hand to fiction writing. Those initial first few pages took on a life of their own and grew into the novella that you see before you now.

A believer of hard work in all aspect of his life; he has started a podcast: - www.facebook.com/socialdistanceinn with a group of friends. He also runs his own sports coaching business and website www.workitoutfitness.co.uk. The goal is to eventually help get kids interested in sports to give them something to focus on; to use fitness as a means of discipline and put them on a better path. This worked for Victor as a troublesome teenager.

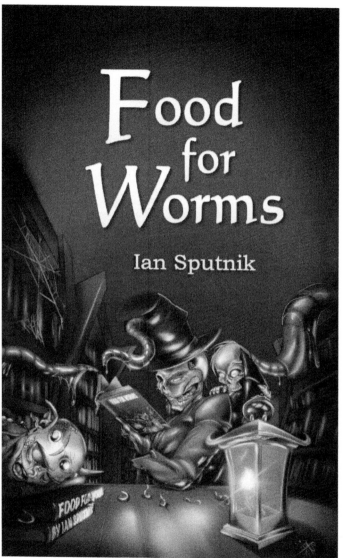

Food
for
Worms

Ian Sputnik

An anthology of small dark bites of life, death,
everything in-between, and beyond.

Printed in Great Britain
by Amazon